USBORNE
QUEST
of the
GODS
D0260299

With thanks to Adrian Bott

First published in the UK in 2012 by Usborne Publishing Ltd.,
Usborne House, 83-85 Saffron Hill, London EC1N 8RT, England.
www.usborne.com

Illustrations by Jerry Parris

Map by Ian McNee

A CIP catalogue record for this book is available from the British Library.

ISBN 9781409521068 JFMAM JASOND/12 02356/1

Printed in Dongguan, Guangdong, China.

Curse of the Demon Dog

Dan Hunter

The Prophecy of the Sphinx

The Sphinx am I
Guardian of the Pyramids
Keeper of Secrets

The past I remember
The present I see
The future I foretell

When the Pharaoh shall die
At the hands of his son
A plague shall fall upon Egypt

The Lord of Storms will rise again
The good Gods will be chained
And monsters will walk the land

The Sacred River shall slow and dry
The sun will scorch the land like fire
The streets of Egypt shall run with blood

But hope will come from the south
A hero of the wheatfields
A king without a kingdom

The last of his family
A lost child of Horus
He shall battle the monsters to free the Gods

He will claim the White Crown
He will claim the Red Crown
He will rule all Egypt

The Sphinx am I
These secrets I share
Guard them well

Manu's Map of Ancient Egypt

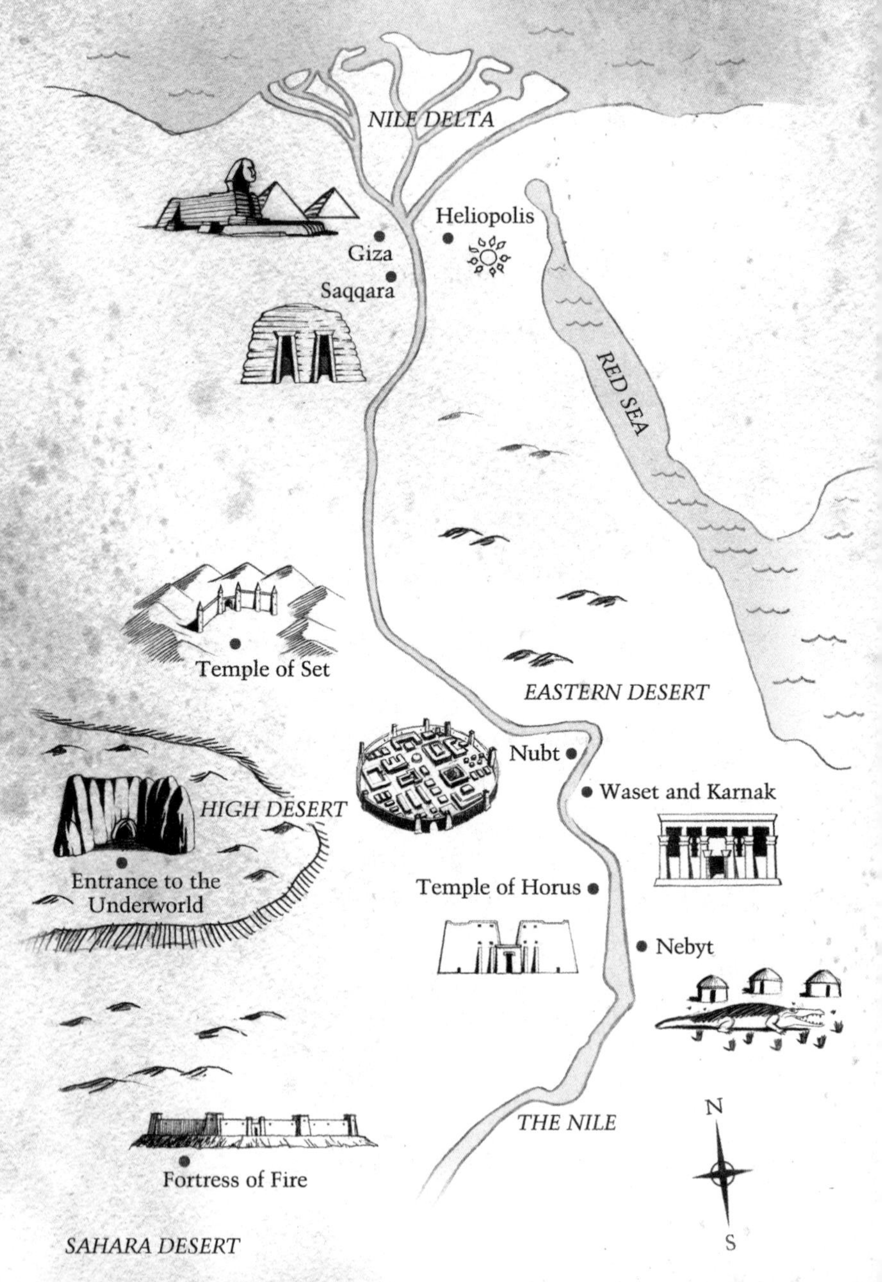

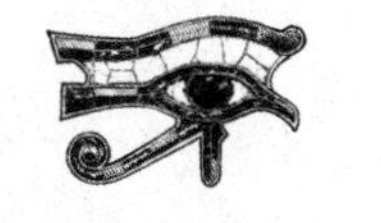

Prologue

It had taken the royal sculptor ten long months to carve the statue of the last Pharaoh. The wise, kindly face had looked out over the throne room for years. But now the new Pharaoh, Oba, took only seconds to destroy it. With a scream, he threw his whole weight against the statue of his dead father, sending it flying. When he had poisoned his father he'd thought all Egypt would be his. He had not thought for one moment that he would face such a challenge to his authority. Slaves and scribes ran for cover as the statue shattered on the floor. The scar-faced priest, Bukhu, winced as alabaster shards flew through the air. He winced again as Oba began to shriek at the top of his voice.

"The Snake Goddess Wadjet was defeated, and now the Sun God Ra is free? How dare you bring me this news?"

"But, Your Majesty—" Bukhu began.

"The God of Darkness, Lord Set, imprisoned the five good Gods so that evil could reign," Oba interrupted. "And now you tell me one of them is free. You're nothing but a filthy traitor! I should have you whipped!" He grabbed a ceremonial staff and snapped it across his knee.

"I am telling you the truth, Your Majesty," Bukhu replied smoothly. "The boy Akori managed to release Ra. I do not like it any more than you, but if I told you comforting lies instead, I would be failing in my duty as your most loyal servant."

Oba ignored him and hurled the broken staff at the young slave girl waiting to anoint his feet with scented balm. She dropped the jar and fled, weeping.

"But you told me Akori was nothing but a low-born brat raised on a farm," Oba said, slumping down onto his throne, panting and red-faced. "Wadjet was a Goddess! How could he possibly have beaten her?"

Bukhu spoke very slowly. "Remember the Prophecy of the Sphinx, Master. It foretold that the challenger to your throne would come from the lowly wheatfields. But Akori could not have acted alone. He must have had help. Help of a most powerful kind."

A flash of fear showed in Oba's eyes. "He has allies? Who? I must know more."

Bukhu smiled a sly smile. "Shall I kindle the Typhonian Flame, Your Majesty? Our Dark Lord Set will have the answers we seek."

Oba's eyes widened. Then he nodded in agreement.

Crossing to the brazier that stood in the middle of the room, Bukhu sprinkled black powder over the glowing coals and muttered a magic spell. Immediately, the fire flared a fierce red. With a sound like distant thunder, a cone of smoke whirled up, filling the throne room with stifling darkness.

In the smoke, a face took form. It was a face of nightmares – a long-eared, long-snouted beast, like some horrible combination of a donkey and a wild boar. Its tiny red eyes gleamed with anger.

"Set!" squeaked Oba, scurrying behind his throne, unable to face his master's rage. Bukhu threw up his hands as if Set were about to blast him with fire.

"M-my Dark Lord," Bukhu stammered, "we ask for your help..."

The throne room grew as dark as a crypt,

and the hideous face of Set loomed out of the smoke.

"IDIOTS! YOU DARE TO ASK FOR MY HELP? WHEN YOU HAVE ALREADY FAILED ME?"

Ripples of red lightning shot out of the smoke cloud and crackled across the marble floor. Oba watched in horror, gripping the back of his throne, certain Bukhu was about to be devoured. And he would be next...

"Forgive us, Lord Set," begged Bukhu. "All is not lost. Four Gods remain trapped and we can easily defeat this farm boy."

Set's voice sank to a low growl.

"Fools! You have no idea of the threat that we face. That 'farm boy' is of royal blood! And he bears the mark of my own greatest enemy!"

"Horus?" gasped Oba.

The terrible face glared right at him, and

Oba realized – too late – that he had spoken the hated name of the leader of the good Gods aloud. That was forbidden in Set's presence. Oba felt the powerful, invisible force of Set's anger squeezing his throat, and he whimpered in fear. He struggled to think of the right thing to say.

"But...My Lord...you...imprisoned him! Surely...your power...is...greater!"

"Yes," Set hissed, letting Oba breathe again. "I am stronger than he is. But even my *power cannot stand against all the good Gods of Egypt acting together. If Akori manages to free them all, I will be defeated – and so will both of you!"*

Oba and Bukhu exchanged guilty glances. Bukhu bowed his head in shame.

"Lord of Storms, we will not fail you again," he said. "Lend us your aid, so we can bring you this Akori's dead body."

"Help us, My Dark Lord," echoed Oba, praying he would not be choked again.

"Very well," rumbled Set. "Since you have failed to find the boy yourselves, I shall send you someone who can – Am-Heh, the Hunter. Nobody has ever escaped him, and even the Gods fear his mighty claws. What Am-Heh hunts, he catches. And what he catches, he destroys."

As he spoke, Set's face faded from the smoke, and a new shape began to grow there. A tall, lean figure with the head of a fearsome hunting dog. An ancient hunger burned in his eyes, a hunger that could never be satisfied. His teeth were bared, and foaming drool ran from his muzzle. Oba grinned. Now this was power!

Am-Heh stepped from the smoke. The curved claws of his feet clicked on the floor. He crouched, as if ready to spring, *and looked up at Oba.*

"What is your bidding, Great Pharaoh?" he growled.

"Find the boy called Akori," Oba commanded. "And destroy him."

Am-Heh gave a ghastly howl. Far off in the depths of the palace, frightened slaves paused from their duties and silently prayed to the good Gods for protection. Only a horror from the Underworld could make a sound like that.

Am-Heh bowed once and raced out of the room.

Oba watched him go, a twisted smile upon his lips. Am-Heh certainly looked hungry! Oba pictured the farm boy Akori lying on a silver platter with Am-Heh looming over him, his terrible teeth bared. His own stomach began to rumble.

"Fetch me my supper, Bukhu!" ordered Oba.

The thought of Akori meeting his end between Am-Heh's huge jaws had given him quite an appetite…

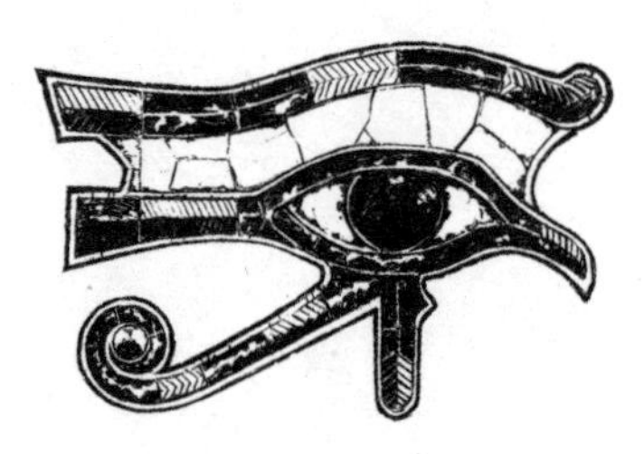

Chapter One

Akori plunged his spear into the rushing water but yet again the fish evaded him. "In the name of Horus!" he exclaimed. "The river is too fast. We'll never catch supper at this rate."

Perched on the rock next to him, his friend Manu broke into a grin. "You should be proud, Akori," he said. "If it hadn't been for you, the Nile would never have flooded again. You've saved our whole country from starving." Crouched alongside them, with her own spear poised, Ebe nodded in agreement. Her wild, tangled hair was wet at the ends from the river's spray.

Akori frowned. He may have saved all Egypt from starvation but right now he felt hungrier than ever. He leaned over to jab at the silver streak of a passing fish and the golden amulet hanging around his neck swung forwards and glinted in the sunlight. Akori was instantly reminded of the adventure he and his friends had recently shared. The adventure that had led to the Nile's flood.

When Ra, the Sun God, had been imprisoned on his own magical sun-barge by the evil God Set, the barge had gone off course, causing a dreadful drought. Together with Manu and Ebe, Akori had defeated the terrifying Snake Goddess, Wadjet, and freed Ra, setting the sun-barge back on course.

The grateful Sun God had given him the amulet as a reward and had promised Akori that it would help him in his quest to free the four other good Gods imprisoned by Set. As Akori wondered which of the Gods he would have to set out to rescue next, the falcon-shaped birthmark on his arm started to tingle. He hoped that Horus, the leader of the good Gods, would find the strength to send a message to him soon.

Akori looked back down into the river. It had been a few days since Ra had been released. Now the swollen Nile was as broad as a lake, and as powerful as an ocean.

Akori saw another shimmer of silver streak through the water and plunged his spear down. The spear shuddered. When he pulled it back out, a huge perch was caught on the end.

Ebe waved her arms about in excitement

and Manu grabbed his net. "It's big enough to feed the entire temple," he cried as Akori dropped the fish into the net.

Akori grinned. "It had better be – it took us all day to catch it!" He felt a pang of sorrow as he thought of the person who had taught him to fish. His Uncle Shenti had taught him so many things when he lived on his farm. It was hard to believe he would never see him again. But Shenti had been killed in an attack on the farm by the evil Pharaoh Oba's scorpion-riding warriors. If only Akori had got to him in time – he might have been able to save him.

Akori was wrenched from his sudden gloom by Ebe. She was still waving her arms about, but she wasn't smiling any more. She was looking worried.

"What is it, Ebe?" Akori asked, wishing that the servant girl were able to speak.

Ebe pointed a little further along the water.

"The boat!" Akori exclaimed.

When they'd set off on their fishing expedition they'd taken a little reed boat across the river to where the fish were more plentiful. They had pulled the boat up onto the bank to stop it from drifting off, but the waters were rising so fast the boat was afloat again and starting to drift away. If they didn't catch it they would be stuck on the wrong side of the Nile...

Akori tried to run across the rocks to get to the boat, but they were too wet and he started to slip and slide. He wasn't going to make it in time! But then suddenly Ebe raced past him. With a great spring, she leaped from the rocks into the little boat, causing it to rock wildly. Some water splashed up, and Ebe yelped. Pulling a face, she paddled the boat back to the others.

Akori climbed in to join her, laughing at her sour expression.

"What's the matter, Ebe? Don't you like getting wet?"

Ebe looked at him as if to say, *I'd rather eat a plate of sand.*

"Well done, Ebe," puffed Manu as he finally reached them, struggling under the weight of the huge fish. He hauled the fishing net into the boat and clambered in after it. Then they set off across the shimmering water. The sun was setting but Akori could still see the Temple of Horus in the distance. He couldn't wait to tell the kindly old High Priest about his catch. During the drought food had become very scarce and the priests in the temple had had to survive on meagre rations of barley and wheat. The Nile had practically dried up and fish had become a luxury.

As they neared the other side, Akori spotted three figures moving along the bank of the river. It looked as if they were heading for the little jetty where the temple boats were tied up.

"Look," said Manu. "Some of the priests are coming to greet us."

Akori stared at the figures. Something about them looked...*wrong*. They moved too jerkily for normal people, staggering and lurching forwards as if they were ill – or dazed.

Akori turned to Manu.

"I'm not sure they are priests," he said.

Manu looked closer. "You're right," he agreed, sounding worried. "There's something very strange about them."

Akori nodded grimly. "I think we'd better row a bit faster."

Manu and Akori heaved at the oars,

determined to reach the jetty before the strange figures did. Their pace soon began to pick up, but then Ebe started pointing wildly to the shore. Akori saw to his horror that the people on the bank had increased their speed too. And now there were more of them. Ten at least, all moving rapidly alongside the river, waving their arms menacingly at the boat.

"I think they're after us!" he gasped.

"We have to get to the temple," replied Manu urgently. "We'll be safe there. Row!"

The two boys doubled their efforts. The boat raced across the water and soon knocked against the jetty. The three friends scrambled ashore.

"Shall we tie the boat up?" Manu asked. "We don't want to lose it again."

Akori glanced along the riverbank. The figures were only a little way away now.

Their skin was as grey as smoke and they were lunging forwards with outstretched arms and gaping mouths. As they drew closer a terrible smell wafted down to the water.

"Never mind the boat!" said Akori, reaching for the golden *khopesh* sword that Horus had given him. Hopefully its magical powers would work against these gruesome people. "Let's get to the temple!"

They abandoned the boat and ran up the jetty steps. Akori reached the top first. There in front of him stood one of the strange figures. His eyes were dark, sunken holes and his feet were scabbed and rotten. Akori felt fear surge through him. Who were these people? What was wrong with them? And what did they want? One thing he knew for certain, from the way the man was glaring at him, was that they did not want to be friends. Akori glanced back down the steps at Manu and Ebe. "You go to the temple and warn the High Priest." He brandished his *khopesh* at the gruesome figure. "I'll see them off."

"No!" Manu exclaimed as he hauled the fish up the steps and came to stand beside Akori. "We can't leave you alone with them."

Ebe nodded vigorously in agreement and took her place at his other side. Akori felt a sudden burst of gratitude for his friends.

In front of them the grey-skinned people all gathered together as one, like a foul-smelling thundercloud.

"What do you want?" Akori asked, gripping his *khopesh* tightly.

The ghostly crowd started softly chanting.

"What are they saying?" Manu whispered.

Akori shook his head and frowned. "I don't know. It sounds like 'dare'."

"Dare?" Manu echoed.

Ebe drew her lips back and hissed at them. But the figures only lurched closer and chanted louder.

"Akori?" Manu whispered.

"Yes."

"I don't think they're saying 'dare' at all."

"No?"

"No. I think they're saying—"

But Akori didn't need Manu to tell him, he'd worked it out for himself. The figures were chanting "death". His heart began to pound but he knew he couldn't look afraid. He stared into the sunken eye sockets of the middle figure and raised his *khopesh*. He was ready if they decided to attack. "Who are you?" he asked. "Where are you from?" The ghostly man threw back his head and let out a hollow laugh. All of the other dreadful figures started to laugh too. The foul smell grew stronger. It was worse than the smell of fish guts left out to rot in the sun. Then the man stopped laughing and looked straight at Akori.

"Shhhhh," he hissed.

Akori frowned.

"Shhhen," the man hissed again.

Shhhen? Akori glanced at Manu and Ebe but they both looked as puzzled as him.

"Shhhhennnnnnntiiiiii," he gasped, lurching towards him.

Akori took a step back in horror. Shenti! It couldn't be? Could it? He stared at the man's ragged clothes. They were streaked with dirt and full of holes, but as he looked at them more closely they did seem oddly familiar. The man lunged forwards again. Akori tried to grip his *khopesh* more tightly but the palm of his hand was slippery with sweat.

"Shhhennnnnntiiiii," the man hissed,

stretching his arms out as if about to strangle Akori.

Ebe took a step closer to Akori.

"Use your sword!" Manu urged. "Kill him quickly, before he kills you."

But Akori shook his head. "I can't."

Manu stared at him in shock. The foul-smelling crowd of figures lurched forwards, chanting, *"DEATH! DEATH! DEATH!"*

"What do you mean, you can't?" Manu cried as the trio started edging backwards along the jetty.

"It's my Uncle Shenti."

Manu's mouth gaped open in shock. "But your Uncle Shenti's dead."

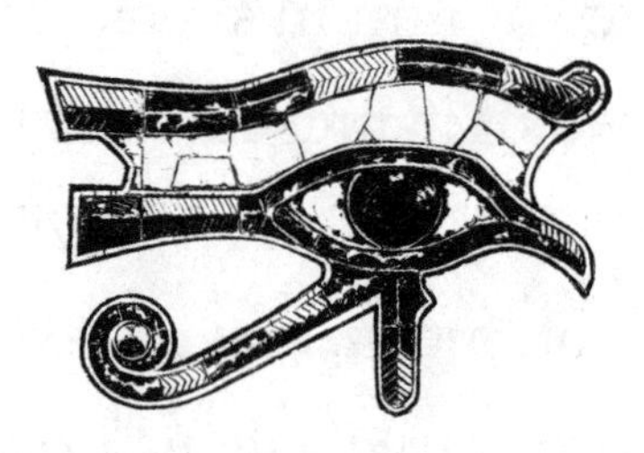

Chapter Two

Akori grabbed the fishing net from the floor. "Come on!" he cried, swinging it over his shoulder. "Let's go along the riverbank. We have to get to the temple to protect the High Priest." The trio jumped down from the jetty and started running along the riverbank towards the temple, their feet squelching and sliding in the thick mud. Although he didn't dare look back, Akori knew the ghoulish people were close behind; he could feel their foul-smelling breath upon his neck.

"But if your uncle is dead then how can he be this...this thing?" Manu panted as he stumbled along beside him.

"I don't know," Akori replied. He heard a loud thud from behind him and turned to see Ebe had tripped and was scrabbling about in the mud.

"Ebe!" Manu cried as the ghouls closed in on her like a dense river mist.

Summoning all of his courage, Akori flung down the fishing net and let out a roar. To his surprise the figures actually stopped chanting for a moment and hovered motionless in a circle. Seizing the opportunity to strike, Akori charged at them, slicing the air with his *khopesh*. All he had to do was imagine he was back on the farm where he used to live, harvesting the crops. As long as he didn't think about what he was really hacking down he would be fine.

The *khopesh* sliced into the first figure and a terrible high-pitched moan rang out across the river. It was like slicing through a rotten melon. Horrible smelling juices splattered out across the riverbank. The other ghouls all turned their sunken eyes upon Akori. And this time when they started chanting it was deafening. *"DEATH! DEATH! DEATH!"*

"Run, Ebe!" Akori cried.

Ebe picked herself up off the ground. But instead of running away she leaped onto the back of one of the gruesome figures and started hitting it over the head. It began thrashing about, trying to shake Ebe off, but the harder it flailed the tighter Ebe clung on. Akori marched towards another of them, sweeping his *khopesh* like a scythe. The ghoul looked at his wounded companion lying on the floor and it started to back off. Akori felt a rush of confidence – now it was afraid of *him*. He turned and looked at the hideous man who had said he was Shenti. Could the haggard grey figure in front of him really be his dead uncle? It didn't make any sense. Once a person died they went straight to the Underworld, didn't they? His heart pounding, Akori took a step towards the man, holding his *khopesh* aloft. The man raised his ragged arms, stared at Akori through the sunken hollows of his eyes, and then turned and started lurching off down the riverbank the way he had come. Seeing him go, the other ghoulish figures all turned and followed. Ebe ran over to join Akori and Manu.

Manu shook his head in disbelief. "By the ring of Isis, that was close," he sighed.

Akori nodded and put his *khopesh* back in his belt. "We must go to the High Priest and tell him what has happened."

Ebe brushed herself down, Akori picked up the fishing net and the trio began making their way up the narrow path between the storehouses that led to the temple. Every few steps they would turn and look anxiously over their shoulders, but the figures had drifted off without trace.

By the time they reached the temple the sun had set. The only light came from the flickering torches standing sentry-like on either side of the huge wooden door. As they made their way up the wide stone temple steps the door swung open with a loud creak and the frail High Priest shuffled into view. "Akori? Manu? Ebe? Is that you?" he enquired, his unseeing eyes staring out into the dark.

"Yes, it's us," Akori called, running over to greet him. "Are you all right? Has anything happened while we've been gone?"

The High Priest frowned and shook his head. "No. I was starting to worry about you though. You've been gone so long. Did you manage to catch anything?"

"The river was stronger than the mighty Bull God Apis," Manu explained. "It took us all day to catch one fish."

The High Priest's face fell.

"But it's a huge fish," Manu added. "Nearly as big as a house. Akori caught it with his spear."

"That's not all that happened," Akori said, taking hold of the High Priest's thin arm and starting to walk back into the temple. "High Priest, we have encountered something terrible on our way back from the Nile."

The High Priest froze in his tracks. "Where is Ebe?" he asked, his voice filled with concern.

"She is here," Akori reassured him.

Despite the fact that Ebe had disobeyed the High Priest by leaving the temple to join Akori and Manu on their last adventure, he had quickly forgiven her. Ebe was his favourite slave girl and it was obvious to everyone in the temple that he viewed her as more of a member of his family than a member of staff.

Ebe hurried over and took hold of his hand. The High Priest touched her wild hair and beamed with relief. "Pray tell me more," he said, turning his cloudy eyes back to Akori. "Are you all right?"

"Can we go inside first?" Manu asked, nervously glancing over his shoulder into the darkness.

"Yes, of course." The High Priest led them all into the huge temple entrance hall. Akori pushed the heavy door shut behind them.

"They were like nothing of this world,"

Manu began. "They were all grey and lurching and their smell was worse than the smell of death itself. And that's what they kept chanting – 'death, death, death' – over and over again and—"

The High Priest raised a gnarled hand. "Manu, my boy, slow down. I cannot keep up. Ebe, why don't you take the fish to the kitchen so that the cooks can prepare supper? We shall retire to the main hall and then you can tell me what has happened. Slowly."

Scooping the fish up in her wiry arms, Ebe bounded off along the passageway leading to the kitchen. Akori, Manu and the High Priest set off along the arched corridor to the main hall. As Akori passed the rows of giant animal-headed statues on either side he remembered the first time he had come to the temple, shortly after his Uncle Shenti had been killed. He frowned. Had that really been Uncle Shenti he had seen earlier? He hoped the High Priest might be able to provide some kind of answer. His eyes alighted on a picture on the wall. It was of the good God Horus preparing to fight the evil God Set. Akori felt a stab of fear. Had Set himself sent those horrible creatures to kill them?

They entered the main hall and sat down on a bench at one of the long wooden tables. Although the hall was lined with burning torches, Akori couldn't help shivering. There was a definite chill in the air.

"So tell me what happened," the High Priest said as he settled into his chair.

Akori took a deep breath, and began telling him the terrible tale. When he had finished, the High Priest shook his head.

"This is what I have been dreading," he said gravely.

"What do you mean?" Akori enquired.

The High Priest turned to face him across the table, his expression now deadly serious. "As you know, Set captured five of the good Gods."

Akori nodded.

"One of those Gods is Anubis, the Guide of the Dead."

Akori stared at him for a moment. "The Guide of the Dead? But if he is imprisoned how will the dead get to the Underworld?"

The High Priest shook his head gravely. "They can't. The souls of those who have recently died will not have entered the Underworld as they should. They will still be among us! This is what you must have witnessed today, on the riverbank."

Dread churned in the pit of Akori's stomach. "One of the figures that we saw said he was my Uncle Shenti," he whispered.

"His dead Uncle Shenti," Manu added, reminding the High Priest.

"Then that confirms it," the High Priest replied gravely. "Those who have died are still walking among the living."

Akori frowned. "Dead souls walking the earth? But surely you priests can deal with that," he said, trying to sound hopeful. "You understand how to lay the dead to rest, don't you? I thought that was what priests did! You make offerings and talk to spirits all the time!"

The High Priest gave a sorrowful smile. "I wish we could, young Akori, I wish we could. But only Anubis himself is capable of taking the dead to their rightful place."

Akori felt an instant pang of remorse. "I'm sorry. This is my task, not yours." He felt a tingling in the birthmark on his arm as he remembered his destiny. The tingling began to spread throughout the rest of his body. Maybe Anubis would be the next God he had to release, so that the dead souls could be taken to the Underworld and Egypt would be safe. And just as he had saved Ra, he would not fail in his quest. If only Horus could find the strength to let him know. He placed his hand upon the High Priest's arm.

"I just don't know what to do next."

"You expect too much of yourself, Akori," the High Priest replied, smiling gently. "No man is born knowing all he needs to know. Sometimes we must ask others for help."

"But who can I ask?" Akori gazed up at him anxiously.

"Perhaps if Horus hears your plea he will find the strength to come to you," the High Priest said.

He pointed to a shadowy figure at the end of the hall. Akori stood up and approached it.

Once he got closer he could see that it was a statue of Horus, the falcon-headed God of Light, standing with his arm upraised. In his hand was the *ankh* cross, symbolizing the power of life.

Akori felt disappointed. Last time he had spoken to Horus, it had been very different. Then, the God had appeared to him magically, but now he seemed very far away. Even so, all Egyptians believed that the spirit of a God could enter every one of his statues. Perhaps Akori could reach Horus through this one.

He kneeled in front of the statue.

"Mighty Horus, Lord of Light," he began. "Please hear me! You helped me once before – now help me again, if you can!"

For a moment, nothing happened. Then slowly the statue's face began to glow. The light grew stronger and brighter until it was blazing like the desert sun. As if in answer, the falcon-shaped birthmark on Akori's arm began to blaze too. Akori raised his hand to his eyes to shield them. Then, as he watched in amazement, the eyes on the statue's falcon-like face blinked, and its powerful beak moved. Akori heard Manu gasp behind him. The statue was coming to life!

"Hail, Akori," said the voice of Horus.

Akori bowed his head in respect.

"Your victory against Wadjet was hard earned," said Horus. "I salute you and your brave companions. Indeed, you have chosen them *very* well." For a second, a twinkle of amusement showed in the God's fierce eyes, then it was gone. "But there is no time to rest," Horus continued. "It has taken all of my energy to answer your plea and I don't have much time.

I must tell you of your next quest."

Akori nodded. "What must I do?"

"I have discovered that Anubis is being held captive in the Great Pyramid. If he is not released with all haste, the dead will be left to roam Egypt, bringing harm to the living."

"But why would they want to harm the living?" asked Akori.

Horus shook his head. "Until they reach the Underworld, the dead cannot enjoy the good things of life as they used to. They will smell food they cannot eat, see houses and possessions they cannot own, watch people take simple pleasures they cannot enjoy. They will first become jealous of the living, and then angry. And then they will take their revenge."

Akori remembered the figures from the riverbank. He thought of the horrible look of hate on their sunken faces, and shuddered.

"Only Anubis can stand in the way of the dead and their terrible anger," said Horus. "Only he can bring peace to their troubled souls. He will soothe them and guide them, as a good hound guides lost sheep back to their fold. But he cannot do this unless you release him. Until Anubis is free once more, nobody in Egypt is safe!"

Chapter Three

The golden light began to fade from the statue until it was ordinary stone once more, leaving the God's final words echoing around the hall.

Akori's earlier doubt and fear seemed to fade with the light. He felt excited now. There might be danger ahead, but at least he knew where to go to confront it – the Great Pyramid itself!

He turned back to the High Priest.

"I know what I need to do," he began, "I

know where I have to go to find Anu—"

But before Akori could continue, a terrible howling noise rang out. It was coming from outside the temple. It sounded like many voices crying out in hunger. Or rage. "What was that?" he asked.

"It's just the desert wind," Manu replied, looking at the High Priest anxiously. "Isn't it?"

Akori hastily made his way back to join them at the table.

"I don't know," the High Priest replied, his brow creased with concern. "Perhaps it is the wind. Since the floods came it has been very stormy—"

But then a loud pounding noise echoed along the corridor and into the hall, interrupting the High Priest. It was swiftly followed by the sound of running footsteps. Ebe burst into the hall. Beneath her wild mass of hair her dark eyes were filled with fear. She pointed frantically back along the corridor towards the temple entrance. "What is it?" Akori asked. "What is making that noise?" Ebe ran over to them and started tugging on Akori's arm. He took his *khopesh* from his belt.

"Do you think it might be the…the creatures from the riverbank?" Manu whispered.

Akori nodded gravely. "Horus said that the dead would try to bring harm to the living. We must stop them at once."

Akori prepared to leave but the High Priest raised his hand.

"Wait!" he commanded. "If it is the souls of the dead then you have to be prepared. The only thing they fear is fire."

"Fire?" Manu echoed.

The High Priest nodded.

Akori looked at the torches blazing away on the wall. "Quick," he said, gesturing to Manu and Ebe to follow him. They each grabbed a torch and Akori took an extra one, which he handed to the High Priest. "High Priest, go and join the other priests in the living quarters. Don't worry, we will protect you."

The High Priest smiled at him weakly before hurriedly leaving through a small door at the back of the hall. The terrible howling noise grew to a roar, followed by a resounding crash.

"They've broken through the main door!" Manu exclaimed.

Gripping their torches tightly, the trio raced from the hall. An icy cold draught rushed up the corridor to greet them. Ebe turned to Akori and wrinkled her nose. Akori sniffed the air and his heart sank. The corridor was filled with the same horrible smell from the riverbank. Up ahead he saw something move in the shadow of one of the statues. He put his finger to his lips and gestured at Manu and Ebe to follow him quietly. The three friends began tiptoeing up the hall.

Just as Akori drew level with the statue, a thin grey arm shot out of the gloom and grabbed onto his tunic. Quick as a flash, Ebe thrust her torch at the figure and a piercing scream rang out. It was followed by a puff of foul-smelling smoke and the figure disintegrated into a pile of dust. But before Akori had the chance to thank Ebe, more grey, withered arms started appearing from behind the other statues and other figures lurched into view. *"Death, death, death!"* Their chant echoed along the passageway. *"Death, death, death!"*

Akori gripped his torch tighter. He didn't care how many ghouls appeared, there was no way he was going to let them win, not when all of Egypt was at risk.

"Come on!" he yelled to the others, raising his torch aloft. Then he charged at the figures. Manu and Ebe followed hot on his heels, copying Akori as he swung his torch from side to side.

One by one the foul figures disappeared in puffs of smoke. And one by one new figures kept on coming, their vile smell and evil chants filling the passageway. As Akori glanced at Manu and Ebe battling away valiantly beside him he felt a glow of pride. There was no way the ghouls could win against them. But then disaster struck.

Manu lashed out so vigorously at one of the ghouls that his torch flew from his hand and crashed to the floor. The flame sputtered

and died. Quick as a flash, one of the ghostly figures descended upon Manu. Ebe raced to his aid but in her hurry tripped and fell, dropping her own torch. Instantly Manu and Ebe were surrounded by cackling ghouls, all of them with their arms outstretched, reaching for Akori's friends' throats. They were going to strangle them! Akori lashed at the foul creatures with his torch, but the flame was too weak to deal with so many at once. He heard Manu calling for help from somewhere deep within the grey, stinking mass.

"Don't worry," Akori called back. "I will save you."

But how could he save Manu and Ebe with only a weak torch? In desperation Akori made a silent prayer to the good Gods to help him. Almost immediately he felt the amulet around his neck begin to burn and the flame on his torch exploded into a sizzling golden-white light. Akori remembered the words Ra had uttered when he had given him the amulet: "It will bring you light, no matter how dark your path seems."

Holding the Talisman of Ra in his free hand, Akori lashed out with his blazing torch at the figures surrounding his friends. The figures hissed and wailed and began to skulk back into the shadows. To Akori's huge relief, Manu and Ebe came stumbling towards him.

"Come on!" Akori called. "Get your torches, we've got them scared." Manu and Ebe picked up their torches and Akori relit them from his own. As they backed the figures into a corner, Akori was reminded of how he used to round up the sheep on his uncle's farm. He raised his torch to examine the sunken faces gaping back at him but there was no sign of his Uncle Shenti. With all of their torches now burning so fiercely, the three friends soon managed to turn all of the foul-smelling figures to dust. As soon as they had gone Manu hurried to shut the huge temple door that was now gaping open and creaking in the breeze.

"That was close," he said with a sigh. "I thought they had us then for sure."

"Let's go and check on the High Priest," Akori said. The others followed him back through the main hall and along the narrow passageway to the living quarters. They found the High Priest sitting in his private chamber, gripping a torch in his gnarled hands.

"Akori, is that you?" the old man asked, staring at them blindly as they entered the room.

"Yes, don't worry, you're safe now," Akori replied.

"Was it them? Was it the souls of the dead?" the High Priest asked. "Had they broken into the temple?"

"Yes, but we saw them off," Akori told him, gently taking the torch from the priest's hand and placing it in the holder on the wall.

"You should have seen our torches," Manu exclaimed. "They burned as brightly as the mighty Ra's sun-barge!"

"Well done," said the High Priest. "Now you must prepare for your next battle – releasing Anubis from the Great Pyramid. But not before you have eaten and slept."

Akori looked at him, shocked. "But with the souls of the dead on the loose, surely we must leave immediately?"

The High Priest shook his head. "The battle you have ahead of you is going to require all of your strength and wit, young

Akori. You need to rest first. And besides, starting your journey to the Great Pyramid will be a lot safer by daylight, when the souls of the dead are at their weakest."

"But what if more of the dead come and get us while we sleep?" Manu asked anxiously.

"As long as you keep a torch burning beside your bed they will not come near you," the High Priest reassured him. "And I will put some of the strongest priests on guard outside your doors."

After a slightly nervous supper of fish stew, Akori made his way back to his bedroom. Manu and Ebe went to their own rooms further down the corridor.

Placing a torch right beside his bed, Akori hoped for dreamless sleep and welcome rest. But as soon as he fell asleep dreadful images filled his mind. He dreamed that something ancient and terrible was pursuing him. He could feel its hot breath on the back of his neck it was so close. Then he was wading through deep mud and could hear a panting sound, closer and closer, and the beat of his own heart thudding.

He knew he must not look back. If he did, he would see the thing that was chasing him, and he would be lost. But he could not stop himself. As he struggled through the mud, he slowly turned his head. And there, right behind him, reaching out with its terrible claws, was—

Akori moaned and rolled over in his sleep.

Now he was dreaming of his Uncle Shenti's farm. The buildings were burning, and the laughing scorpion-riders were coming for him. His Uncle Shenti was calling out to him desperately. *Akori! Akori!*

Akori mumbled, pulling the blanket over his head.

The smell of smoke was in his nostrils. Hot flames licked at his skin. His uncle was still calling out. His hoarse voice was very close now. *Akori! Akori!*

All at once, Akori woke up with a gasp. He was covered in cold sweat. The torch beside his bed had gone out. The room was filled with darkness, and as he lifted his head, Akori gasped in terror.

Standing at the foot of his bed and staring at him with terrible sunken eyes was the shadowy figure of his Uncle Shenti!

CHAPTER FOUR

Uncle Shenti stretched out his arms and began to make his way up the bed towards Akori. Shenti's face was full of anger. Akori tried to sit up, but felt himself being pushed backwards. He was being pinned to the bed, held down by his Uncle Shenti! He tried to breathe in, but the pressure on his chest was too great. He felt as if he were drowning.

Uncle Shenti sneered down at him through black, lifeless eyes. Akori tried to beg for mercy, but could only make a strangled choking noise. Coloured spots danced before his eyes. He was going to die. When Manu came to find him in the morning, there would be a cold corpse lying in the bed. But just as Akori felt himself slipping into bottomless darkness, a strangely ordinary sound came from outside. It was the crow of a cockerel, announcing that morning had come.

At that very moment, a pale finger of sunlight reached into the room and fell upon Akori's amulet. A brilliant white light reflected forth and Uncle Shenti fell backwards as if dazzled. Choking and spluttering, Akori grasped the amulet and pointed it at his uncle. Shenti staggered backwards, towards the window and frantically clambered out. The way he was cringing and wincing, it was as if the sunlight was burning him.

Akori struggled among the sheets for a moment, gasping and trying to calm his wildly beating heart. As soon as he felt able to stand, he got out of bed and ran past the sleeping guard outside to Manu's room.

"Akori?" said Manu sleepily, sitting up and rubbing his eyes. "Is it time to leave already? Just a minute. I'll get my scrolls..."

"Uncle Shenti!" Akori panted. "In my room!"

Manu woke up fully. "What? Dead Uncle Shenti?"

"Yes!" Akori exclaimed.

Ebe padded soundlessly into the room, carrying a lamp. She greeted Akori with a frown of concern.

Manu stared, horrified. "You mean..."

Akori nodded. "He wasn't with the others last night. He must have hidden somewhere in the temple and waited until I was asleep.

He tried to kill me! But I managed to fight him off, and he escaped through the window."

"Thank the Gods," Manu said, rummaging in his bag for one of his countless scrolls. "Don't worry, Akori. Once we have freed Anubis he'll take all the dead souls back where they belong."

Manu unrolled a scroll and pointed to a picture of a God with the head of a jackal. He was standing in a cavern, at the head of a procession of stooped-over, pale figures approaching a huge dark archway.

"The entrance to the Underworld," Manu explained. "When you die, Anubis is there to meet you. He takes away all your fear, sorrow and anger, and leads you to the land of the blessed dead."

Ebe took one look at the pictures and stepped back with a shudder. Akori was surprised. Ebe was the bravest of the brave, but something about the jackal-headed God seemed to make her uneasy.

"When Anubis is free once again," Manu continued, "all the lost souls will be able to carry on their journey. Your Uncle Shenti will go where he belongs, in the company of the good Gods."

"Are you sure?" Akori asked. "He wasn't always very… I mean sometimes he…"

"He was not a good man? Is that what you are saying?" Manu looked very serious. "Akori, the good Gods are merciful. Eventually, even the worst of men may be forgiven. Only the evil Gods hold grudges for ever and never forgive." Manu rummaged through his bag and unrolled a map. "This is where we must go," he said, tracing a long route with his finger. "It is the way to Giza – and the Great Pyramid." His finger stopped at a black-edged triangle on the papyrus. "If we journey by boat it should only take a few days."

As they packed their bags, Akori thought about what Manu had said about the good Gods showing mercy to everyone. But how could the Gods ever forgive the new Pharaoh Oba, who had sided with Set and murdered his own father? Surely there would be no mercy for him. Akori placed his hand upon his golden *khopesh*. One thing was certain, if he didn't release all of the good Gods, Set and Oba would never be brought to justice. As Akori thought of the enormity of the task ahead of him, his birthmark once again began to tingle, as if Horus himself were reminding him to stay strong.

"Don't worry," Akori whispered, "I won't let you down."

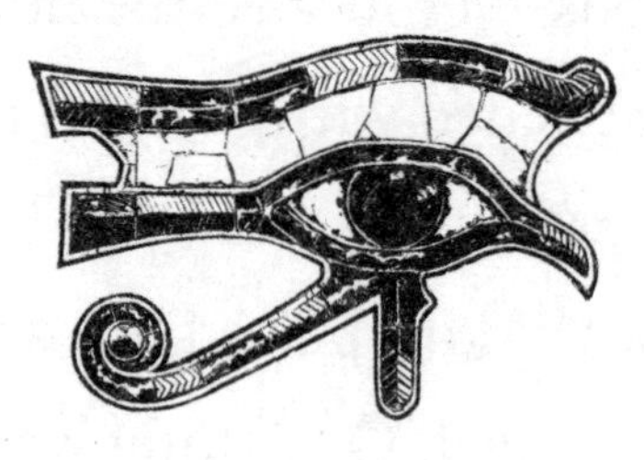

CHAPTER FIVE

After saying goodbye to the High Priest, the three friends set off on their journey. In the bright morning light, everything almost seemed back to normal. The swollen Nile was glistening and the fields were peaceful. But Akori knew that if he could not rescue Anubis, things would never really be normal again.

After a couple of days travelling downriver, their boat sprang a leak, forcing them to continue the rest of their journey on foot.

They tracked through the endless fields, watching out for any sign of the dead. But all was silent and still. Even the birds made no noise. The only sound was their own footsteps crunching in the dry soil, and Manu's tuneless humming.

Normally Ebe would be racing ahead to scout out the way. But now she seemed nervous, lagging behind and looking over her shoulder, as if she thought something was following them…

As Akori watched, Ebe stopped and sniffed the air. Akori wondered if she could smell the foul stench of the dead again. He took a deep breath in, but all he could smell was black, gooey Nile mud and the warm smell of freshly ploughed furrows. Ebe carried on sniffing and looking worried. Something had definitely spooked her.

Manu had obviously noticed this too.

"Cheer up, Ebe! We're going to the Great Pyramid. Haven't you ever wanted to see it? I know I have."

Ebe made a *harrumph* noise, and shrugged.

"It's a magnificent sight, I've been told," Manu went on. "It's the tallest building in the whole world. Can you imagine that?" His face took on a dreamy look. "The pyramid is covered with limestone blocks, smooth and white as alabaster! I can't wait to see it, shining white on the horizon, like a man-made mountain..."

It might be white on the outside, but I bet it'll be black as the Underworld on the inside, Akori thought. His heart began to pound as he contemplated the unknown dangers ahead of them. There was no way Set would have left the imprisoned Anubis unguarded. The question was, which of his evil servants would he have chosen for the job? Akori decided not to share his thoughts with his friends. Ebe looked worried enough as it was.

"Let's stop for a quick bite to eat," Akori suggested.

They all sat cross-legged on a rocky shelf overlooking the Nile and shared some bread and sheep's cheese. As Akori was beating the dust out of his sandals, Manu pointed out a group of people on the opposite bank, moving down to the water's edge.

"Look, Akori!" Manu cried. "The farmers are going back to work."

Akori smiled. "Of course they are. That's what farmers *do.* Didn't you know? If there's work to be done, we just get on with it, no matter what."

"No matter what, eh?" Manu laughed, taking a bite of cheese.

"You trainee priests don't have a clue how the world really works," Akori joked. "Even if there are monsters and the dead roaming the earth, *someone* has to bring the wheat and barley home. The work won't do itself." He threw a loaf at Manu, who caught it. "Do you think bread lands in your lap by magic?"

Ebe shook her head and made a sad noise in her throat. She was staring over the river. Manu followed her gaze and stopped mid-chew.

Akori's smile vanished too. The figures Manu had thought were farmers were lurching and staggering away, their arms outstretched.

Akori put his sandals back on and stood up. "Let's get going. I've lost my appetite and we have so far to—"

But before he could continue, Ebe leaped to her feet, hopping on the spot and making terrified, gabbling noises. Akori reached out, trying to calm her, but she pushed his hands away, panting heavily.

"Ebe, what's the matter?" he asked.

She pointed behind him and gestured wildly. Then, with her two hands in front of her face, she mimed great jaws snapping, hooking her fingers like gnashing teeth.

Akori and Manu turned to look.

At first they saw nothing. But then Akori noticed a figure on the horizon. It was moving so fast it was kicking up a dust cloud behind it.

"It's probably just a rider," he said. "Or a chariot. Whatever it is, it's a long way away."

But Ebe wasn't convinced. She pointed again, more desperately than ever. Akori looked back. Whatever was causing the dust cloud, it *was* far away. He frowned. But was it his imagination, or was it already growing closer?

Akori felt a nervous tingle run down his spine. Ebe let out a growl of frustration. Then she turned on her heel and started to run.

"What do we do now?" Manu wailed.

"We follow her, of course!" Akori exclaimed. "Come on!"

The two boys raced after Ebe, who was already far ahead of them. But she didn't show any sign of stopping, or even slowing down. Akori glanced back over his shoulder and gasped with shock. The dust cloud was closing in fast! How could anything move so quickly? It had grown huge too.

"Faster!" he yelled, putting on a fresh burst of speed.

Manu gasped and struggled under the weight of his bags. Akori began to panic. Ebe was too far ahead, and Manu was falling too far behind!

Then Manu stumbled and fell. Akori dashed back and pulled him to his feet, but they had lost time, and now the cloud was closer still. Akori could hear a strange panting, snarling noise coming from it, like some huge wild animal.

Grabbing Manu's bags, Akori led him around a bend in the river, where green rushes waved in the sunlight. Akori knew ground like this could become boggy and treacherous. It might slow their pursuer down, but if they put a foot wrong, they'd be stuck fast too!

All at once he remembered the dream he'd had about struggling through mud while something terrible chased after him. Was it about to come true?

Akori glanced over his shoulder and what he saw nearly made his heart stop.

It was the enormous figure of a man. But

where the human face should have been was the head of a savage hunting dog, its tongue lolling as it ran, its fangs bared and glistening in the sunlight…

In a minute or two, the dog-headed monster would catch up with Akori. Those teeth would make short work of his flesh and bones. There wouldn't be enough of him left for a decent burial.

Akori ran for his life.

By his side, Manu was screaming something that sounded like, "Come here! Come here!" Akori frowned. No – it was "Am-Heh! Am-Heh!"

Am-Heh? The words didn't make any

sense, but there was no time for Akori to try and work them out. He had to keep running!

Ebe was still sprinting ahead, vanishing around a bend in the path where it passed a rocky outcrop. Seconds later, Akori heard her give a muffled shriek of panic.

He and Manu raced around the bend after her. The dog-headed horror was almost upon them. Akori could hear its feet thundering on the ground.

As they rounded the bend, Akori saw Ebe flailing her arms madly. She had sunk into the ground right up to her waist!

"Quicksand!" Manu shouted.

Akori sprinted forward and grabbed both of Ebe's arms. If he could pull her out before she sank too far, there was still a chance of saving her. He heaved backwards as hard as he could.

Was that his heart pounding in his ears, or the sound of approaching feet? He couldn't tell.

The quicksand dragged at Ebe's body with a hungry slurping noise but, with Manu's help, Akori managed to pull her to safety.

Ebe immediately struggled to her feet. She tugged at Akori, trying to break free from his grip. Clearly, she wanted to keep on running but Akori wouldn't let go. She glowered as if she were about to bite him.

"No, Ebe!" Manu hissed. "Over here, quickly." He dived off to the side and hid behind a boulder.

Akori quickly realized what Manu was thinking. The rocky outcrop would hide them from view, and the monster would come charging round the corner, too fast to stop – just like Ebe. They could use the quicksand as a trap.

Together, he and Ebe threw themselves off the path. They rolled to a halt behind the boulder with just seconds to spare.

The three of them held their breath as the dog-headed beast ran right past them. Dust flew up into their faces. Then they heard a wet splash and a sudden yelp of surprise.

The dust settled, and they peered cautiously over the boulder. Now they could see their pursuer clearly for the first time. It was stuck in the quicksand, gnashing its dog-like jaws in frustration and sinking slowly but definitely down.

It splashed its arms in the muck and gave a mournful howl.

"Yes!" Manu yelled. "We got him."

"Let's not start celebrating yet," Akori warned. He still felt the lingering terror from his dream. Was the creature really trapped?

Cautiously, he approached it. The monster

had sunk up to its chest, but being stuck in the quicksand had only made it angrier. The fearsome creature glared at him and gave a low growl. Akori swallowed hard.

"What *is* that thing?" he asked, looking at the struggling beast.

"His name is Am-Heh," Manu replied. "The Hunter God. Legends say he never fails to catch his prey."

"Well, it looks like even the legends can be wrong sometimes," Akori said, trying to sound like he believed it. "Let's get out of here."

They continued a short way, but just as they were about to round a bend, Akori glanced back to where Am-Heh was trapped. A terrible sight stopped him in his tracks.

Am-Heh was lying flat in the sand. He had flung out an arm and sunk his long fingers into the firmer ground at the edge of the quicksand. Now he was trying to pull himself out of the sucking mire. Powerful muscles flexed in his arms as he dragged himself slowly up and out.

"Oh no," stammered Manu, backing away. "Oh *no*!"

Am-Heh let out a terrible snarl as he hauled himself up with his mighty arms. He was halfway out now.

Akori, Manu and Ebe backed off to the very edge of the swampy ground. Akori drew his golden *khopesh* sword. He could only hope it would be enough of a weapon against this unstoppable terror.

With a roar and a mighty heave, Am-Heh dragged his whole body free. Then he squatted on his haunches, shook himself like a dog and stood to his full height.

Before, he had been terrifying. Now, he truly was a living nightmare. His body was

oozing with sandy slime. His dreadful teeth were bared, as if ready to feast on young, tender meat.

Akori took a deep breath and brandished his *khopesh*. "Get back!" he yelled.

Am-Heh cocked his head and gave an evil grin. Akori glanced around in panic. On one side was a wall of rocks – on the other, the river Nile. And behind them was more quicksand! There was nowhere left to run…

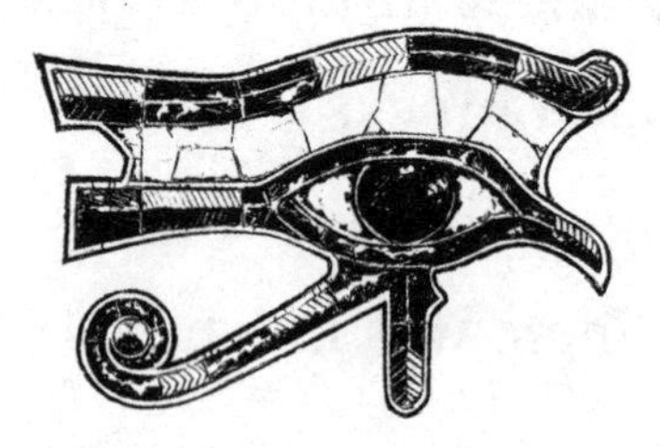

Chapter Seven

Akori looked across the river, blood pounding in his ears. There was only one place they might be able to shelter – a lumpy-looking island a little way out into the river.

"Swim for it!" Akori shouted, pointing to the island with his sword. "I'll hold him off for as long as I can."

Ebe was already moving. She darted past Akori and splashed into the water with a yowl of fear and disgust. As soon as she was deep enough, she began to swim towards the island.

"Manu, you too. Get away from here," Akori yelled.

Am-Heh swung an arm towards Akori, trying to knock him sideways, but Akori leaped out of the way just in time. A clawed hand whooshed past his face, missing it by a hair's breadth.

"My scrolls!" wailed Manu as he stared out at the river. "I can't get them wet. They'll be ruined!"

Am-Heh snarled and glared at him. Then he surged towards Manu, snapping his jaws hungrily.

Akori quickly jumped into Am-Heh's path with his *khopesh* raised. Behind him he heard a loud splash. Akori glanced over his shoulder and saw Manu plunging into the river after Ebe, holding his scroll bags above his head. Now only Akori and Am-Heh were left on the riverbank.

Am-Heh lunged, aiming a bite at Akori's neck. This time, Akori swerved his body to one side and slashed out in a desperate counter-attack. The razor-sharp *khopesh* went whistling towards Am-Heh's own exposed throat. Am-Heh dodged out of the way just in time.

He warily circled around Akori, touching his neck as he did so. There was a little bald patch where the *khopesh* had struck. It had come close enough to slice his fur away! Am-Heh looked at Akori with a mixture of hate and wariness.

Then he crouched on his haunches and leaped through the air, his huge, heavy body hurtling right towards Akori!

Akori stumbled backwards into the river. Cold water washed around his feet. Am-Heh landed in the water with an almighty splash and roared in anger.

Akori glanced back over his shoulder once more. Out in the river, Ebe and Manu were scrambling desperately onto the island. Akori saw Manu frown in puzzlement as he pulled himself onto its bare surface, hauling his soggy bags up behind him.

Was Manu still worried about his scrolls? No – he was poking at the island's surface as if there was something not quite right about it.

Suddenly, the whole island lurched and titled sideways! There was a booming roar from beneath the water and a huge head loomed up out of the river, its nostrils flaring, its immense mouth yawning open to reveal teeth that were longer than swords.

The shock of the sight left Akori weak at the knees. It was a giant hippopotamus – a truly colossal one!

Akori spun around. Am-Heh took a giant

step through the water towards him, looking angrier than ever.

Akori quickly turned back to the hippo. Water streamed from its back as it rose out of the river, with Ebe and Manu still clinging on. It was so huge it was like watching a *house* lift itself up.

Akori spun back round to look at Am-Heh. He was shaking the water from the fur on his head. Then he tipped his head back and gave a mighty roar.

Akori felt terror rise in his chest as he glanced back and forth between the Hunter God and the hippo. There was no escape.

Then, suddenly, Akori had an idea. "Manu, Ebe, jump!" he cried, gesturing at them to dive into the river. As soon as his friends had splashed down into the water, Akori waved at the hippo. "Hey!" he shouted. "Over here you overgrown river-cow!"

The hippo's piggy little eyes caught sight of Akori. With a furious grunt, it charged towards him. At the same moment, Am-Heh gave a menacing growl and rushed forward.

Gritting his teeth, Akori held his ground as the two monsters thundered closer. Then, at the last moment, when the hippo's gaping mouth was so close he could have jumped in, he leaped to the side, plunging into the deep, fast-flowing river.

Behind him, there was an earth-shaking crash and a blood-curdling yowl of pain as the two beasts collided. Next moment, there was a wild frenzy of roaring, snarling, snapping and growling. As Akori came up for air, he tried to see what was happening.

The hippo was lashing this way and that, battering Am-Heh with its massive head. The dog-headed God snarled in mindless

rage as he fought back, tearing at the hippo's thick hide with his huge claws.

But then suddenly the hippo reared up and brought its whole body crashing down on top of him. Am-Heh vanished in a muddy fountain of Nile water.

But where were Manu and Ebe? Fighting to keep his head above the surface, Akori swam towards the spot where he had last seen them. Finally he saw them swimming across the river, trying to reach the far bank.

"We've done it!" Akori gasped as he drew level with them. "We've escaped!"

"Not yet we haven't," spluttered Manu. "We've got to get across the river first, and I don't know if I can swim much further."

Even Ebe was struggling against the strong currents.

"Keep going!" Akori urged, but even as he

spoke he could feel his own arms and legs getting heavy.

Then all of a sudden a chilly mist began to descend on the river. Akori shuddered. The cold waters of the Nile seemed to be draining all of his energy. Looking across at Manu and Ebe, he could tell they were feeling exactly the same. Manu didn't even seem bothered about his scrolls any more – his bags dragged behind him in the water.

But just then, as if it were a sign from the Gods, the prow of a boat emerged from the mist.

"Look," Akori shouted, pointing at it with a weary arm. "Let's see if they can help us."

They forced a last effort out of muscles that burned with pain. The boat drew closer.

Akori saw the silhouette of a man leaning over the edge of the boat. He was holding out an oar for them to grab on to. They were safe.

The three of them clambered aboard and landed in a bedraggled heap in the bottom. Nobody spoke. For a moment they just lay there, taking huge breaths, glad to be alive. Then Akori looked up to thank their rescuer.

But his words died in his throat. The head that peered down at him was on back to front! Akori stared at the strange figure. The man began to smile at him, but that somehow only made it seem worse.

Manu looked horrified. "Akori...do you know who this is?"

Akori shook his head.

"His name is Aken," said Manu, his voice weak with fright. "He's one of Anubis's helpers."

Akori was puzzled. "But that's good, isn't it? Anubis is on our side. Maybe Aken can take us to him."

Manu gave a hollow laugh. "It's not that

simple. Aken only knows one route, and it's a one-way voyage. He is Anubis's ferryman. He carries the spirits of the dead to the Underworld – where they must stay for ever!"

Manu turned to Akori, his face ashen with fear. "He is taking us to the Underworld. We will never make it back alive."

CHAPTER EIGHT

"So *that's* why he was so glad to see us." Akori shuddered. "With Anubis imprisoned, Aken can't have had any passengers for a while." He shook his head slowly as the awful truth dawned. "So we're to be taken to the land of the dead, while the dead roam the world of the living!"

"Some say that's how the world itself will end," whispered Manu. "Everything gets turned upside down."

The mist closed around the barge, growing

as thick as a grave-shroud. Off in the distance, Akori heard a horribly familiar growling, then splashing noises and howls of frustration. Somewhere, Am-Heh was still searching for them. Ebe gave a shudder and crouched down in the bottom of the boat, as if she was trying to hide.

From beneath them came a deep gurgle. Then the whole barge lurched downwards. Akori sprang to his feet.

Clutching the rail, Manu stared down at the water. Bubbles were streaming up to the surface. "It's starting!" he said grimly.

"What do you mean?" Akori demanded. "What's starting?"

"As the sun goes down, the boat sinks too," Manu explained. "Down to the caverns of the Underworld!"

Akori could just make out the sun through the mist. It was a feeble red, and vanishing fast. Another gurgle and another lurch. They were definitely lower in the water now.

"Aken!" Akori yelled, tugging at the figure's robe. Although Aken's body was facing them, his head was facing the other way. "Please stop! Take us back! We need to save your master Anubis!"

But Aken just kept rowing, his head turned away, as if he hadn't heard.

"It's no good, Akori!" Manu shook his head. "Dead souls beg Aken to turn back every single day, but he can't. He can only do what he was created to do. He has to take this same voyage, day after day, until the end of time."

Sinking into the Underworld as the sun set…it reminded Akori of something. He punched his fist into his hand as he remembered. Of course! Ra's sun-barge did the same thing! Akori grasped the Amulet of Ra and held it aloft. Manu had said Aken could only do what he was created to do. He wasn't evil, he was just simple, so maybe he could be fooled...

"Help me, Ra," he prayed. "Please help me!"

At once, a bright golden light blazed out from the talisman, shining in all directions. In an instant, the mist thinned and vanished, burned away by the warm light.

Aken looked over his shoulder. For a moment, he looked surprised and deep in thought. Then he shrugged and kept rowing. Slowly the boat began to rise back up in the water.

Ebe leaped to her feet and gave Akori a huge grin.

"It's working!" Manu whispered. "Aken thinks it's still daytime!"

The barge glided silently up the river,

Akori's talisman shining out like a beacon. He looked up at the darkening sky, and wondered how long they could fool Aken. But Aken just kept on rowing, until eventually a huge white pyramid loomed into view on the horizon.

"Look!" Akori said excitedly. "Over there, across the sand dunes. It's the Great Pyramid."

"But we still have one problem," said Manu. "How do we get to the shore? Aken's not going to steer us there, is he?"

Akori's brow furrowed as he stared across the river. He hadn't thought of that. Luckily, Ebe knew what to do. Quick as a panther, she leaped onto Aken's back and clamped her hands down over his eyes.

Aken bellowed and tried to shake her off, but she clung on tightly. Akori grinned. This was more like the old, courageous Ebe!

While Aken was distracted, Akori snatched

one of his oars and plunged it into the water. The river was flowing so fast the current nearly swept the oar from his hand, but Akori held on. Leaning heavily on the wooden shaft, he used the oar like a rudder, steering the boat towards the shore. In a matter of minutes, it thudded into the bank and Akori, Manu and Ebe leaped out.

Watching from the boat, Aken scratched his head in confusion.

"Thank you, Mighty Ra," Akori whispered. As he spoke, the light from the talisman faded and darkness descended once more. Aken blinked, and suddenly seemed to come to his senses. Seizing his oars, he rowed swiftly back into the middle of the river. Then, as Akori watched, the barge began to sink lower and lower into the water. Soon it had vanished into the murky depths of the Nile, along with its strange ferryman.

Akori tucked the Talisman of Ra back inside the pouch at his waist and sighed gratefully.

"I've never been so glad to feel dry land under my feet." He turned to the others. "Come on, there's no time to lose. We have to save Anubis before the dead take over the living."

They hurried across the sand dunes towards the Great Pyramid. As they ran, two more huge triangular structures emerged on the horizon. The three gigantic pyramids towered over them like a mountain range, glowing white in the moonlight. Suddenly, Manu gasped.

"Look!" he breathed. "The Sphinx!"

There, crouched in front of one of the great pyramids as if it was guarding them, was a massive stone statue. It had the body of a lion but the head of a king, staring out across the desert with blank eyes.

Ebe's face lit up with delight. Filled with new energy, she raced down the dune ahead of them and soon reached the foot of the huge stone creature. She rubbed her face gently against it, like a cat saying hello. Akori followed her and gazed up at the huge stone face, solemn and regal in the moonlight.

The birthmark on his arm was tingling. Akori knew that the Sphinx was connected to his destiny. When he had first arrived at the temple, the High Priest had shown him the Prophecy of the Sphinx, inscribed in an ancient block of sandstone. It had foretold his quest.

"A hero of the wheatfields," the Sphinx had called him. *"He shall battle the monsters to free the Gods."* As Akori gazed up at the ancient stone face he was sure the Sphinx was smiling at him, as if

he still had some secrets left to tell.

Beyond the Sphinx stood the Great Pyramid. Akori thought of Anubis trapped somewhere inside the giant stone structure and the breath caught in the back of his throat.

"We need to get inside," he said, turning to Manu. "I don't suppose any of your scrolls would tell us how?"

But before Manu could answer, a mournful groan echoed across the dunes. Ebe gave a warning growl, but Akori already knew what that sound meant.

Rising over the top of the nearest dune came a seething mass of grey lurching figures. It was full of snarling faces, outstretched arms and clutching hands. The dead! Not just a few this time, but a whole *army*.

"Quick, Manu, how do we get in?" demanded Akori.

Manu began delving through his scrolls, but many of them had turned to mush in the river. The ghastly army of the dead had staggered over the top of the dune and was now sweeping down the other side like a dark wave. In less than a minute they would reach the Sphinx…

"Manu, we have to hurry."

"I'm trying my best," Manu snapped, pulling out yet another damp scroll. As he unrolled it, it tore down the middle.

Ebe yowled and pointed. Hundreds of empty-eyed figures were now charging towards them.

"I know, Ebe, I know." Akori readied his *khopesh.* It would be a hopeless fight, but he wasn't going to give up without one.

Just as Akori was about to charge towards the dead army, Manu shouted in triumph.

"Found it," he yelled. "In the scriptures of

Ta-Nech, it says there's a secret door in between the Sphinx's paws. Akori, *we're right on top of it!"*

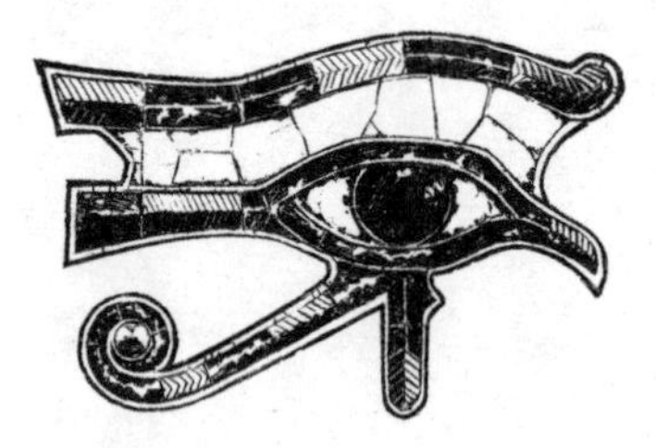

CHAPTER NINE

As the dead surged towards them, Akori, Ebe and Manu quickly ran between the Sphinx's huge paws. There they found a sloping stone surface, covered with weathered hieroglyphics.

"The scrolls didn't mention this!" said Manu. "One of those symbols must be a clue to the way in. But which one?"

Akori felt desperate. He couldn't even read hieroglyphics! And if they couldn't get in, Anubis would never be freed.

But then he noticed a familiar shape in among the rest. A falcon, with its wings spread. He knew it well by now – it was the same as the birthmark on his arm. The symbol of Horus. The Pharaoh's Mark...

"This one!" he said, and jabbed it with his thumb. With a deep grinding noise, an ancient panel in the stone slowly began to open.

The lurching army of the dead was now almost upon them, shrieking and wailing.

"Hurry!" Akori called, as the stone panel continued to edge its way open.

"They're going to get us!" Manu cried. "We're too late."

"Let's pull it," Akori shouted.

All three of them kneeled down and tugged at the heavy stone. The panel juddered and opened a fraction more, just wide enough for them to fit through.

Without a moment to lose they jumped down into the darkness.

Akori looked up, and saw a sea of angry dead faces glaring down at him. Then the grinding noise began again and the panel closed. They found themselves in pitch blackness.

"How did you close the door?" Manu asked, impressed.

Akori swallowed. "I didn't."

They felt their way along in the darkness. They were in a passageway that went downwards at first, then levelled out, before angling upwards again.

"We must be under the Great Pyramid by now!" Manu whispered after a while. Ebe nodded in agreement. Akori's heart began to beat faster. Hopefully they would soon be within reach of Anubis. But then he heard something.

"Shhhh," he said to the others. "Did you hear that?"

From further down the passageway came the distant sound of voices chanting. And a faint glimmer of light.

Cautiously they made their way to the end of the passageway. It emerged into a gallery that looked down on a vast chamber. Narrow stairs led downwards. Huge flaming torches on the walls bathed the room in a fiery glow.

The chanting was much louder now, and Akori gave a start as he saw where it was coming from. Dozens of figures filled the chamber below. But these figures looked different to the ones outside. Instead of being clad in dirty raggedy clothes, they were wrapped in layer upon layer of dusty bandages.

Mummies!

"They must be the dead who were

mummified just before Anubis was captured," Manu whispered. Akori nodded.

Around and around the chamber the mummies marched, repeating the same words:

"Never let him go," they chanted. *"Never let him go..."*

"They must be talking about Anubis. Set must have ordered them to guard him," whispered Akori, peering around in the flickering light. A huge black sarcophagus lay in the centre of the chamber. The mummies were circling it. With a shudder, he realized that Anubis must be lying helpless inside the sarcophagus. But how were they going to reach him?

Manu was shaking all over. "I'm sure there's some way we can avoid those mummies," he whispered. "There's got to be something in the scrolls! A word of command

to make them run away, or a spell to turn them back to ordinary mummies again…"

But as Manu crouched down and started to unpack his bags, disaster struck. One of his scroll holders slipped out of his hand and started to roll away. Ebe tried desperately to snatch it back, but it was too late – reaching the edge of the gallery, it tipped over and fell with a clatter into the chamber below!

The chanting stopped.

Akori, Manu and Ebe exchanged frightened glances and crouched down in the shadows at the back of the gallery.

Then the chanting began again, louder and more angry than before. Akori could hear what they were saying now, and his heart plummeted.

"Death to the intruders!" came the dry, rasping chant. *"Death to the intruders!"*

Chapter Ten

"Get ready to fight!" Akori hissed as he raised his *khopesh*. "Unless we free Anubis, the undead will be swarming all over Egypt!"

Ebe crouched down, teeth bared, eager for battle. But Manu still kept searching frantically through his scrolls.

"There's got to be a better way," he insisted. "A safer way."

"Manu, we don't have time!" Akori exclaimed. *"They're coming to get us!"*

The mummies were chanting louder and

louder as they reached the foot of the stairs and began to tramp upwards.

Akori brandished his *khopesh* and stepped onto the top stair. "Ready, Ebe?"

She nodded grimly. Manu however, stayed in the shadows and carried on searching through his bags.

Stiff, dead arms that had broken free of their bandages reached up the stairs towards Akori. He summoned up every bit of courage he could and, with a loud battle cry, he charged down. Ebe screeched and sprang along beside him.

The *khopesh* struck, and sliced the arms right off the first mummy. It staggered, then fell off the stairs and landed with a dusty crash. Akori stared after the mummy. The blow had felt horrible, like chopping through dry sticks.

The next mummy tried to grab the

khopesh and pull it out of Akori's grip, but Ebe kicked the monster hard under the ribs and it toppled over, taking another mummy with it. Waving their arms helplessly, they fell into the chamber, smashing a torch off the wall on the way down. Ebe yowled in triumph. But there were more coming, chanting as their feet stomped up the stairs.

Akori hacked one in half, slammed the sword hilt into another's face, and chopped the leg from another. Dust showered him with every blow. Mummy after mummy went tumbling down into the chamber. Beside him, Ebe lashed out with feet and fists. When one mummy managed to grab hold of Akori, Ebe helped to pull it off.

Akori's arms ached. Ebe was panting heavily. But the more mummies they defeated, the more seemed to appear. He forced himself to raise his *khopesh* and fight on.

But then a mummy moved to strike him and the *khopesh* went flying.

"No!" Akori cried as the sword clattered to the floor below.

He tried to run after it, but it was too late – the chanting mummies were all around him, muffling his mouth, holding his struggling limbs. Ebe came racing to his rescue but it was no good. Yet more mummies swarmed in to form a circle around her and she was captured too.

"What's happening?" Akori heard Manu cry from the gallery above.

"Stay back!" Akori shouted in warning, but it was too late. A stream of bandaged figures surged up the stairs. There was the sound of a brief struggle and then the mummies returned to the chamber holding a wriggling Manu, still clutching his bags.

The mummies carried Akori, Manu and

Ebe to the side of the huge chamber, where some empty sarcophagi were propped against the wall. The mummies lined the three friends up in front of the sarcophagi and then began to march around each of them, wrapping them in something. Akori looked down. *Bandages!* He was being wrapped from head to foot, and so were Manu and Ebe. Akori tried to wrestle free, but there were too many mummies surrounding him.

The tight bandages were being wound around his hands, his legs, his chest. Akori could hardly breathe. *Is this how a fly feels, when a spider traps it in its web?* he wondered. And now they were winding bandages around his mouth – and pushing him inside a sarcophagus.

Akori's heart thundered in his chest as panic gripped him. What a terrible way to die, suffocated inside a sarcophagus. Now he would never be able to free Anubis. He was destined to lie in a tomb for ever, mummified alive!

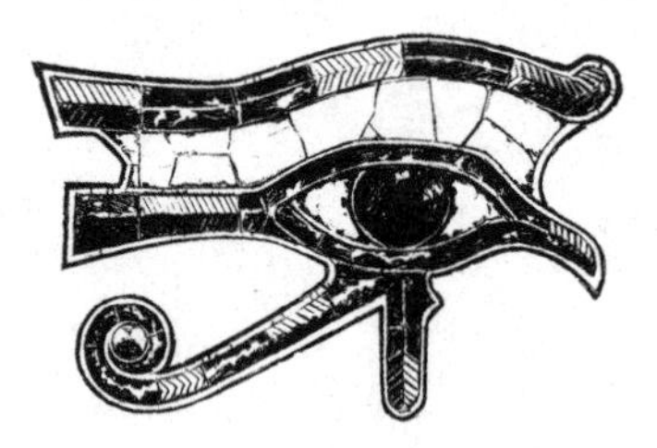

Akori stood upright in the open sarcophagus. He tried to move his hands, thinking he might be able to wriggle free, but the tight bandages held him like ropes. He wished he had his *khopesh,* but it was still lying on the floor where it had fallen, in the centre of the chamber.

It was no use. He had failed. He had let the High Priest down. Worse still, he had let his entire country down. Without Anubis to guide the dead home, Egypt would become a miserable, haunted hell, all because he hadn't fought hard enough. And he wouldn't be able to continue in his quest to save the other three Gods either.

Through a tiny gap in the bandages over his eyes, he could see that the mummies had gone back to marching around and around the huge black sarcophagus. They chanted monotonously as they marched: *"Victory to Set! Victory to Set!"*

Akori shuddered. If Set won, Horus himself would never be freed and evil would reign for ever more.

But then Akori noticed something that made hope leap in his heart. On the wall near his sarcophagus was a twisted, broken piece of metal, left when one of the falling mummies had smashed a torch from the wall. It looked a bit like a hook.

It was risky, but he had nothing to lose.

And that part of the chamber was dark, now that the torch was gone. The shadows might hide him…

Praying the mummies wouldn't notice, Akori took little hops out of the sarcophagus and into the shadowy area. Then he tried to hook his bandages on to the sharp metal prong. It was a tight, difficult struggle in the dark, but finally he managed to attach the bandaging on his back to the jagged hook. Then he tugged, and to his joy the bandage began to come loose!

Akori started to hop round in a circle to unwind the bandage, but soon realized that would take too long. So he took a deep breath and spun on the spot, faster and faster, like a bobbin unwinding thread.

The last of the bandages fell away. He was finally free! But the whole room seemed like it was still spinning. Akori almost collapsed on

the floor before he managed to steady himself. He'd never felt so giddy. He pushed himself up and staggered towards Ebe, as the walls and floor lurched from one side to the other.

Fighting the dizziness that threatened to overwhelm him, he began to unwrap Ebe. Once he had freed her hands she helped him take her remaining bandages off. Akori held a finger to his lips, and Ebe nodded to show that she understood. She gave him a silent look of thanks as she stepped out of the dusty pile of bandages.

Together they took stealthy steps through the shadows towards Manu. Neither of them made a sound.

Working quickly, they released Manu, Ebe's claw-like nails plucking and tugging at the bandages. As soon as his face was uncovered, Manu opened his mouth to speak, but Akori clamped a hand over it.

Leaning in close, he whispered quietly into Manu's ear.

"No talking or they'll hear us," he explained. Manu nodded, his eyes wide.

The mummies' chanting was so loud now it seemed to shake the chamber.

"Victory to Set! Victory to Set!"

Akori looked at the huge black sarcophagus and his heart sank. The lid looked as heavy as one of the Great Pyramid's huge stone blocks. Even if he could somehow find the strength to battle through all of those mummies, how would he ever lift it?

Then he remembered what Horus had said to him, when he appeared to Akori before his first adventure. The *khopesh* was not just a weapon! Horus's words echoed in his mind:

"The blade is enchanted, and will cut through iron and stone...but...it is also a

key...a key to free the Gods, when you find us..."

Akori looked at the *khopesh*, lying on the flagstones where it had fallen. Mummies marched past it in a constant procession. All he had to do was reach it...

The mummies were staring straight ahead. Gesturing at Manu and Ebe to stay where they were, Akori got down on his hands and knees and crept across the floor. As long as he stayed below their eye level and didn't make a sound, he might just be able to do it. Bandaged feet marched past him, round and round. To his horror, he heard the chant change once again.

"Let the dead devour the living."

They were running out of time!

Desperately, Akori crawled forward a little further, then waited for a gap in the marching feet. It was now or never – the *khopesh* was within reach! He grabbed it, and instantly a magical warmth radiated up his arm. Akori slid away from the marching feet with the grace of a sand snake, then crawled back to the safety of the shadows. He had his sword, now he just had to make it to the sarcophagus. But how could he do that with so many mummies in the way?

He glanced over at Manu and Ebe. Manu was rooting around in his bag. Akori frowned. What was he doing? Hadn't those scrolls got them into enough trouble already? Manu pulled out a scroll holder, then grinned at Akori before flinging it across to the other side of the chamber. Akori's heart skipped a beat. What was Manu thinking? Now they would be discovered for sure. The mummies stopped dead in their tracks, mid-chant. But instead of looking at Akori, Manu and Ebe, they turned in the direction of the noise.

Then they started marching over to the scroll holder, chanting, *"Death to the intruders!"* Akori smiled as he realized why Manu had thrown the holder – to create a diversion.

While the mummies were distracted, Akori ran over to the sarcophagus and slid his *khopesh* under the huge stone lid. He started trying to lever it open but the lid was so heavy it was like trying to lift the pyramid itself. Akori pushed down on the *khopesh* with all of his might. "Please help me, mighty Horus," he whispered. The birthmark on his arm began to tingle and heat flowed from it down into the *khopesh*. Akori gasped as the sword began to glow as red as a flame. The lid opened a little. Akori pushed down on the *khopesh* and it was as if Horus himself was pushing too. The lid swung open as easily as if it had been made of bamboo.

A rushing sound filled the chamber, as if

fresh air were suddenly being sucked into it. Every stone in the wall and floor danced with golden light. The sarcophagus was wide open.

Akori took a step back as a stately figure rose up before him. Anubis. He was tall, like all the Gods, and he wore a shimmering cloak that was the colour of a starless night. His skin was brown, and his head was that of a jackal. But his eyes were kind, and he radiated an aura of peace and calm.

Manu stared, speechless and awestruck. Ebe ran and hid behind a pillar. Akori frowned.

"It's all right!" he called to her. "This is Anubis, not Am-Heh!" But Ebe stayed where she was.

The mummies were standing motionless and no longer chanting. As if recognizing their true master, they bowed down before Anubis.

The God looked around the room and made a strange gesture with his hand. The broken mummies that Akori and Ebe had defeated reassembled themselves, and stood up to pay homage with the rest.

"I owe you my thanks, young mortal," said Anubis. His voice was deep, and although he was standing right next to Akori, it seemed to echo, as if he were speaking from a hollow place below the earth. "But other Gods are still in peril and need your help to free them from Set's chains. Let this aid you in your quest."

From his cloak Anubis took a jewel-headed pin in the shape of a scarab beetle, and placed it in Akori's hand. "This is the Scarab of Anubis," he said. "When you or any of your friends are hurt, it will grant you the gift of healing."

"Thank you, My Lord," Akori replied,

bowing his head in respect.

"Now you must go back to the Temple of Horus," said Anubis. "I have much work left to do tonight. This army of the dead must be returned to their proper place, and there are many other souls waiting to be led to the Underworld."

Akori bowed deeply before Anubis. But as he rose, he spotted a familiar figure standing behind Anubis that gave him a horrible chill. His Uncle Shenti.

But as he stared at his uncle, Akori realized something had changed. He didn't look angry any more. In fact, a peaceful smile was spreading across his face. Akori wasn't sure, but he thought his uncle almost looked proud. Anubis placed a hand on Shenti's shoulder and a golden aura shone out around him. Akori shielded his eyes and watched as Shenti looked up at Anubis gratefully and then began to fade into the light until he had completely disappeared.

Anubis smiled at Akori, who was standing open-mouthed in surprise.

"Return to Horus in peace and safety, royal prince," he declared.

It was more than just a blessing. There was powerful magic in Anubis's words. Akori felt the world fall away from under him.

For a few seconds, he was caught up in a whirling, shimmering tunnel of light. Huge shapes flew past almost too fast to see – the pyramids, the Sphinx, the boats on the Nile. He was travelling at breakneck speed, back across the desert sands! It was like flying...

His landing wasn't quite so breathtaking. He fell out of the air in a sprawling heap, down onto soft sand. There were two thumps either side of him and he turned to see Manu and Ebe, landing in exactly the same way.

"Where *are* we?" Manu complained, rubbing his head and clutching his bag of scrolls to him.

"Right back where we started!" said Akori, pointing at the huge gateway of the Temple of Horus. The polished stone shone in the moonlight.

Ebe gave a little cry of delight. She raced up the steps, with Akori and Manu following close behind. They ran into the main chamber so fast that Ebe almost knocked the old High Priest off his feet.

"Ebe!" he laughed, feeling her wild hair and hugging her to him. He looked around blindly. "Are Akori and Manu with you?"

"Yes, we are here," said Akori. He and Manu walked over to him and Akori took hold of his hand. "Our quest was successful – Anubis is free."

The High Priest's face broke into a

beaming smile. "At last! Now the dead will be able to find their way home and the people of Egypt can sleep easier in their beds."

He led them all over to a table and they sat down at the long benches. Ebe laid her head upon the High Priest's shoulder, while Akori and Manu told him everything that had happened.

"You have done exceedingly well, Akori," said the High Priest. "And I am sure the gift of Anubis, with its healing powers, will be of great aid to you in your future missions."

"I wonder when you will have to use it," Manu said as the call sounded for supper and dozens of servants entered the chamber carrying platters of delicious-smelling food.

As Manu spoke, Akori felt the birthmark on his arm begin to tingle. Once again Horus was reminding him of his destiny. But which of the Gods would he be sent to rescue next? Would it be the magical Goddess Isis? Or the mighty warrior Goddess Sekhmet? One thing was for sure, Akori thought to himself as he looked down at his falcon-shaped birthmark. He would be ready and prepared for his next quest, no matter how hard it might be…

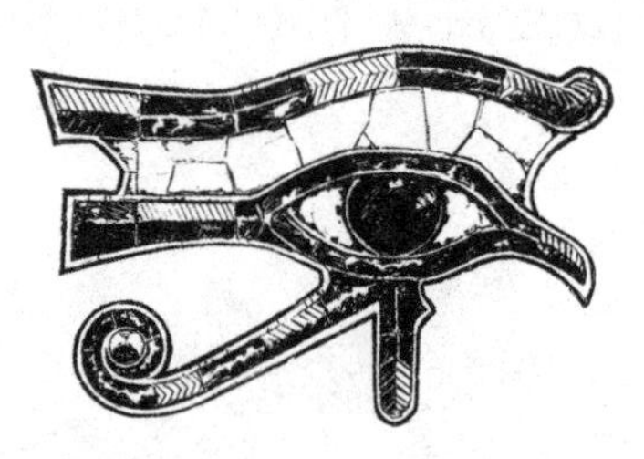

Epilogue

The Pharaoh Oba lay stretched out on a couch in his throne room.

Soft music was playing, a table laden with fruit stood nearby, and Oba was eating grapes from a bunch held up for him by a terrified slave girl. On a couch opposite, his priest and advisor, Bukhu, was sharpening his sword on a whetstone.

Suddenly the music stopped as the muddy, bruised figure of Am-Heh slunk into the room.

He stood, a little unsteadily, by the fruit table. His tail was drooping and his head hung in shame. He looked more like a bashful puppy than a mighty hunter.

"Speak," Oba commanded.

In a whining voice, Am-Heh answered. "My Pharaoh, I have failed you. I found the boy Akori, but...he got away."

"He got away," echoed Oba, clenching his fists in anger.

"There is more," Am-Heh admitted. "The boy somehow entered the Great Pyramid. Even pursued by an army of the dead, he was victorious. Your Majesty...Anubis is free."

"I see," said Oba. He got to his feet. Am-Heh stood waiting, his horrible head bowed.

Oba grabbed a handful of fruit and flung it at him, screaming at the top of his voice.

"Incompetent cretin! Useless cur! Get out of my sight!" *Am-Heh howled piteously and ran out of the room.*

Bukhu stood. "Your Majesty, my friend, be calm!" He laid a firm hand on Oba's trembling shoulder. "Akori and his friends may have succeeded this time, but there is no way they will thwart us again."

Bukhu's face darkened. "I will make sure of that myself..."

DON'T MISS AKORI'S NEXT BATTLE!

BATTLE OF THE CROCODILE KING

Akori must brave the crocodile-infested waters of the Nile to battle two evil Gods – the terrifying Crocodile King, and his gruesome wife, the Frog Goddess – both hungry for his blood...

Akori had never seen so many crocodiles in his life. And there behind them, urging them on, was a colossal figure. Its skin gleamed in the moonlight like pockmarked leather armour.

At first Akori thought it was a huge crocodile that was somehow walking on its back legs, but then he saw the giant had human-shaped limbs and torso supporting its crocodile head. It bellowed an order, and the crocodiles surged forward even faster than before.

He stared in horror. It was Sobek! They'd walked straight into a trap!

ISBN 9781409521075

ALSO AVAILABLE:

ATTACK OF THE SCORPION RIDERS

For his first quest, Akori must risk his life, fighting giant scorpions and a deadly Snake Goddess. But will his terrifying battle end in victory?

ISBN 9781409521051

LAIR OF THE WINGED MONSTER

Vicious vultures and deadly beasts lie in wait for Akori as he searches the desert for the Hidden Fortress of Fire – and the Goddess imprisoned there. Will he survive or will this quest be his last…?

ISBN 9781409521082

SHADOW OF THE STORM LORD

The battle to end all battles has begun. Akori must fight Set, the dark Lord of Storms himself, and beat Oba, the evil Pharaoh, to claim his rightful throne. But can Egypt's young hero finally win the crown?

ISBN 9781409521099

FREE GAME CARDS IN EVERY BOOK!